A SMALL TOWN SECOND CHANCE SWEET ROMANCE

Rescued
BY MY
Brother's
Best Friend

ABBY GREYSON

£2
8/24

Contents

About The Book

The past comes rushing back at the sound of his voice...my brother's best friend and my new next-door neighbor.

Lane Kincaid was my secret crush for as long as I can remember.
He's also the one I had every intention of avoiding when I came home.

But fate had different plans;
I got into a car accident.
And he's the first person to come to my rescue.

As my gaze collides with his, all thoughts flee.
My icy indifference begins to thaw.

He's even more handsome than I remember.
But I must stay away.

He shattered my heart.

Each interaction weakens my resolve,
And puts a dent in my protective armor.

There are times when he looks at me, and my breath catches.
I can't help but wonder if he feels the same.

Now, I'm being rescued by my brother's best friend in more ways than I ever dared to dream.

Chapter 1

Emma

I TURN TOWARD THE sound of knocking on the window, groggily lifting my battered head from the steering wheel it crashed into moments ago. My body struggles to breathe, and the pain shooting along my nerve endings steals my breath. As my gaze collides with the face on the other side of the window, all thoughts evaporate, and I give a wry laugh to the universe that twisted all my best intentions into this ridiculous reunion. Those blue eyes have haunted every dream since puberty hit, and my love for Lane has only blossomed.

This trip has become a nightmare, and I haven't made it home yet!

"Emma, can you unlock the door?" Lane asks as my brother's face pops up next to his.

There they are the dynamic duo of my big brother, Kieran, and his best friend. Side by side, as always.

They are volunteer firefighters in our hometown, and I should have guessed they would be the first ones on this scene. I am the wayward sister, a constant bother, and the introvert to their big outgoing personalities.

Reaching a hand as far as I can, I hit the unlock button with a fingertip. The effort is all I can muster as my lungs scream and pain shoots the length of my leg, still pinned under the dash.

"Oh my goodness, is she dead?" An old man that I don't recognize joins the party of paramedics and firefighters standing guard. I can barely see his shadow from the corner of my eye, but I guess he was the big old Caddy that veered in front of me seconds before I met the tree I was currently resting against.

"I'm not dead," I hoarsely whisper, the effort sending me into a coughing fit.

"I didn't see you coming; I was looking at the deer I swerved to miss," the guy offers back.

Thank you, Captain Obvious! I figured the man hadn't seen me coming around the bend on the country road leading into Briar Glen. I knew this was an unfortunate accident and that the old, backcountry route into town was hardly ever traveled on but by locals. I thought it safer than the highway option, but apparently, I was wrong. Now my entrance to my hometown would not be as low-key as I had been hoping.

"It's okay, Mr. Olson," I hear Kieran say. "Why don't you let these nice men take you to the ambulance and check you out?"

"You sure know how to make an entrance," Lane whispers as he holds my hand and the paramedics brace my neck. "Try to take it easy, and we'll get you out shortly."

I would be a little more relaxed if someone else was attending to me—anyone else on the planet but him. Lane was the person that had kept me from this place for years now, and I had big plans to avoid him as much as possible while settling back into the groove here in Briar Glen. I had missed so much about my childhood home, and the nostalgia finally overcame the glow of the big city. I know coming back is the right move, even if I have to be in the personal space of this amazing human that never had left my heart or mind. Though he doesn't know that, and I intend that to remain the case until they lay me in the ground.

"I just want to make sure everyone knows I'm home," I tell him, deciding on humor to lighten the tension. I start coughing up a storm at the effort that comeback cost me.

"Welcome home," he whispers in that low, gruff tone that I adore. "I would have thrown a different kind of party if I had known you were coming," he says as my gaze finds his.

I have dreamed of this moment for eight years since we last saw each other. In every daydream I've had of our reunion, I was at least standing, usually with a blowout and some fabulous dress on. Bloodied and stuck in a weird position in a now banged-up ten-year-old Toyota on the side of the road was the furthest impression I was hoping to make. I was a gangly high school graduate when our paths last crossed, and lifetimes of experience had put Lane even further from my league.

As they unceremoniously lift me from the battered car, I wish that Lane would carry on helping with other parts of the scene.

"I'm sure we can catch up later," I tell him in dismissal, hoping I might be upright and wearing something not blood-stained the next time we crossed paths.

"I'm going to ride with you." Worry is etched in every crevice of his face. "Kieran has a trainee team and will meet us at the hospital."

I feel a tear sneak down the side of my face. The pain in my leg is becoming unbearable, but I don't want him to see me cry. I know it's dumb and I shouldn't care about such things now, but this person is the epitome of the perfect man. Having him witness me at my lowest point is breaking my spirit. I had been planning the perfect homecoming and how sophisticated I would act when I returned to my hometown.

"How bad is the pain?" Lane asks, bending low to my cheek as they wheel me into the ambulance.

I look at him, worried that I might have said something aloud. That is the thing about Lane and Kieran, though; even as kids, they could understand me better than the rest of my family. Neither of them thought my quiet, introverted nature was anything to poke fun at and instead had long taken to be my voice to the world. He could finish my sentences, fulfill unspoken requests of mine, and settle me with one grin from that handsome mug of his.

"You are one tough cookie, but I know that look," he murmurs, glancing down at my leg.

"How bad does it look?"

"Well, you are definitely going to need a cast," Lane quips.

"You can tell that just by looking at it?" The paramedic gives Lane a warning look. I know he is good at his job, but I can't recall anyone touching my leg.

"Um, I don't mean to say this to freak you out," Lane says, looking apologetic. "The bone might be peeking out through the skin a bit." The look he gave me would have made me belly laugh under other circumstances. However, this was my appendage we were talking about, and that news was not what I was hoping to hear.

"What?" I ask as fresh coughs hit my chest, and I feel light-headed. "That sounds bad," I add as I realize my voice is super unsteady.

I see the ambulance start to spin. Nausea takes hold of my midsection. If I wasn't already lying down, I would need to do so immediately. I can't pinpoint a single issue at the moment, as everything hurts; my stomach is lurching at the movement of the fast-paced ambulance. It takes every ounce of willpower to stay alert.

"Lane," I whisper. "I don't feel so good."

"Well, you look great, even bloodied and battered," he tells me, squeezing my hand. In a haze, I realize he never let it go. When I pivot slightly to glance in his direction, those eyes aren't lying or teasing.

"I missed you so much," I hear myself confess, feeling like I might pass out.

I feel his warm, large palm squeeze mine again. He doesn't say a word as the ambulance lurches forward; that is all my stomach can handle as the contents hurl from my body. I'm pretty sure this can't get any worse, but thankfully I choose this moment to pass out, blocking any other embarrassing moments.

Chapter 2

Lane

I PACE THE LENGTH of the hallway, waiting for Kieran to finish with Emma. The doctors were done with surgery on her leg hours ago and have stabilized it for now. She should be able to go home in a couple of days, but she won't be able to stay on her own. To make matters worse, I have no idea what the plan is. Kieran didn't tell me she was coming, which is pretty strange as we share nearly everything and see each other every day. We run a massive company and are responsible for hundreds of employees; the teeny detail of Emma resurging into our lives may have slipped his mind. Maybe, but I have my doubts.

I spin around as I hear the door opening, and Kieran puts a finger to his lips to ensure I don't speak. He knows he's in trouble with me, but I doubt he realizes the depth of my anxiety at the moment. We walk a good distance down the hall before he faces me.

"I didn't know she would get here today," he starts before I can chastise him.

"Does she know about it all? I know you told me last year you didn't want to tell her until after the book about our company came out. You felt like it would be like rubbing salt in her wounds over the lackluster results from her first book. I thought that was crazy, as Emma's always celebrated your wins in the past, but I went along with it," I mutter.

"I told her I bought a new house," Kieran says as I slug him hard in the arm.

The man does have a gift for understating things.

He adores his sister more than anything and tries hard to never give her a reason to be upset with him. Emma is nearly eight years younger than us and was the apple of her family's eye. She was not as outgoing as us but an introverted, reading, band geek of a kid. I, like Kieran, thought she hung the moon, and we did our best to always make her feel special, even when other kids were not especially kind during those gnarly teen years. Today though, she had grown into those curves and had the most beautiful face. She was not a baby or hormonal teen needing protection from the world, but Kieran still appears to be in that phase of their relationship.

"We bought a block and built two mini-mansions on the property. She is going to figure out that you and I have been hiding stuff from her," I say, running a hand through my hair.

I'd never been this off balance before, but my well-ordered life was crumbling. I've spent years building a business that supports veterans in various roles, and the tiny dream is flourishing. Unfortunately, Kieran had not wanted his sister to know how successful we were, as she was a struggling writer for a number of years. Their parents currently live in Miami, so they visited them there for vacations, holidays, and such over the last few years. That move also meant that I didn't cross paths with Emma. I always made excuses not to travel with Kieran for said events.

I knew it was cowardly, but I figured seeing her regularly was going to do nothing but risk my business partner and the relationships that I hold dear. I had loved Emma for so long, and it was one of those terrible plot twists that I was going to hold close and never reveal to the world at large. Kieran would beat me into a bloody pulp, and it was just a bad idea for so many reasons.

I honestly believed that distance and all the years in between our flirtations as children would have dissipated my feelings. One look into her eyes, even filled with fear after that accident, had triggered a response in me that was positively unbrotherly in all ways possible. I wouldn't have any peace. I need to be on my game about hiding these feelings from Kieran and Emma.

"I think she will be proud of me and you. We give hundreds of vets jobs now and are killing it in the video game arena," he responds, appearing not to understand how momentous a period this is.

"Kieran, your family's home is hers according to what you and your parents worked out. Is that where she's planning to stay during her time here in Briar Glen?" I was not normally someone that got worked up, and the emotional outbursts were more my best friend and business partner's arena. Today though, I felt bad decisions were invading my life, and no one asked my opinion.

"She bought me out," Kieran says, hanging his head. "She wanted to make the place her own and wouldn't just take it. I would guess based on the fair market value number she gave me and the fact that she paid me in cash means she is doing better than I gave her credit for. I think she is returning permanently and wants to renovate and live in the house," Kieran says.

My heart painfully slams against my chest. That house is within a stone's throw from my own, which means that the single most off-limits woman in the world would now be a next-door neighbor again. To make things even trickier, she was badly hurt and would need help. I wonder if Kieran or Emma were thinking about what that would entail. Someone had to get to the house and make certain it was ready for her to live in the downstairs room instead of her bedroom upstairs. It also needed a good airing out.

Emma was a bustling ball of energy who had probably intended on doing the cleaning herself. As she owned the house now, she would most definitely want to update the older decor. The accident would absolutely have put a wrench in those plans.

"I wish you had told me," I exhale as I continue to digest the information being sent in my direction.

"She told Mom and me on a call the other night that city life isn't her jam," Kieran confesses. "You and I know what that's like. She is my sister, for heaven's sake."

"Oh, I know," I sigh. "We need to get over to the house and make sure it will be safe for her with the leg situation."

"I hadn't thought about it," Kieran said. "Any idea of who we can hire from around here? I mean, you and I won't have time to give her the help she needs, and I have back-to-back business trips coming up."

"She's your *sister*," I spit at him, shock spiking my entire body at the horror of him wanting to pawn Emma's care off on someone else.

"We can hire good, well-paid staff to care for her. Lane, we are rich—richer than rich by most standards," Kieran said. "This is what people do in our position."

I know we have the means to see to it Emma is cared for, but it feels wrong. I lost all my family at fifteen; Lane, Emma, and their parents were my only family. I would never leave Kieran to flounder or be cared for by paid personnel if something were to happen. I refuse to allow it for his sister.

"I will take care of it," I state.

"Lane, I promise she will understand," Kieran beseeches me with this look that makes me hesitate.

I just can't do it. Emma being less than a block away, in my town, injured, and needing help, was not anything I was delegating. I don't care what it takes; I'm making sure she is cared for to my specifications.

"I know she will, but my conscience won't let me do it," I admit. "You take care of business, and I'll take care of your sister."

Kieran looks at me firmly, sitting hard on the sofa on the right side of the office. He stares at me longer than is comfortable, and I start to worry about what is going on in that head of his.

"I should have told you she was coming home," he whispers. "I know things were tense with the two of you that last visit home, but I truly thought that was all behind us."

"It was a tough time with all of us growing in different directions," I try to soothe his worry, thinking about the last time I saw Emma.

She tried to kiss me. At the time, she was eighteen and no longer inappropriate to consider dating. I knew Kieran would kill me. So I did the hardest thing I've ever had to do and pulled away from her. The rest of the weekend was tough, and she was gone the next time I went home. We have managed to avoid each other for eight years, aside from the occasional call that Kieran would put me on to say hi.

"I promise I'm just worried about her well-being," I tell him, hoping we can stop talking about Emma now and get back to safer topics.

"Okay, you do what you think is best," Kieran replies, but there is that look he gets on his face with the squished-up eyes and firm set to his mouth that tells me he has more he wants to say. "I have some focus group results for the next game if you want to review them."

We make live-action war games in a host of genres and on a range of apps that allow us to provide different services to support veterans for different forms of therapy and we sell some merchandise. All in all, we have multiple revenue sources that help provide jobs for veterans. The best part is that we get to give back and support a number of causes for our brothers in uniform still serving or recently discharged. It is the best way to honor our service and many others with our post-military work. Getting to work with Kieran and seeing our success to date is just a bonus that I never expected.

"Great, let's review," I tell him, glad to see the conversation switching away from Emma.

I make a note on my phone to head to her house when I'm done for the day. I would make her homecoming much better than it had been thus far. Hopefully, we would have the opportunity to clear the air and reach a close friendship again, as it seems that she will be a neighbor for years to come.

Chapter 3

Emma

I HAVE THIS LITTLE scooter-style device that allows me to move down the hallway, into the kitchen, and even to the workspace where I set up my desk. Thankfully, my laptop did not seem impaired by the crash, so I was already rearing and ready to get back to writing. After getting the largest cup of coffee I could muster from the fancy machine that was on the shelf when I arrived at my childhood home, I make slow progress to my desk.

This place is like a comfortable glove I can slip back into. All my childhood memories flood my brain as I see the pictures that Mom and Dad left when relocating to Miami. I believe they truly felt like they would be back and forth for a while. But these trips never materialized. When I'm feeling better, I'll need to purge the house of things I don't want to keep.

I am so fortunate that the house is mine and that I managed to buy out Kieran's portion. He was unhappy about that little detail and implied I could have it without compensation, but I would never have a single soul believe I took something that was not rightfully mine. After selling the apartment in New York and relocating here, I was able to manage the buyout easily. There was enough left to get some paint, flooring, and other items to give this old house a full facelift.

"Knock, knock," Lane's voice echoes through the space, causing me to nearly spill my coffee. I was not expecting anyone.

"Morning, back here," I call out, as my heart picks up the pace.

I run a hand through my hair and glance down to see a big T-shirt and shorts. Definitely not going to seduce Lane in this outfit that looks like a reject from the donation pile. I hate that I can't do anything about it at this point and honestly want to smack myself for even having the thought. Lane is out of my league and off-limits. I would never risk messing up a friendship like the one he has with my big brother. Besides, I was drinking one weekend years ago to bolster my confidence and shot my shot. He turned away in horror from me and has made sure we are never alone in the same room since. I figure that tells me all I need to know about any chance he reciprocates my feelings.

"Hey, you look like death warmed over," Kieran offers as I just sit and glare at him.

"At least you're upright, and it appears you're getting some work done," Lane says much gentler. "I would imagine showering on your own is challenging?"

"For sure," I tell him, with tears rising. "I haven't figured out how I will manage that yet."

"I can help," Lane says suddenly as all eyes turn in his direction.

I nearly laugh aloud at the expression on Kieran's face.

"I don't think that is advisable. I'm pretty sure you seeing me naked is not something that would be good for our friendship," I tell him, but my heart is pounding a million beats a minute as that visual takes hold of my brain.

"No, I can help in that I found a nursing assistant willing to come in and lend a helping hand. Your brother recommended we find someone when you were in the hospital. I want to be here to help with meals, cleaning, and such, though I did realize that some of the activities you would need the most support doing were not in my purview."

"I can't afford it," I utter. "I have some savings and big plans to work on the house. Additionally, I have an advance coming for my next series, but I think I can figure this out without needing to hire someone right now."

"Stop. That isn't relevant," Kieran said, surging forward. "I took care of the hospital bill, and anything else you need is covered. I told you that I didn't want the money for the house, and now I am able to use it for something you wanted. I think that is me winning."

"You are terrible," I tell him, but I'm so grateful I tear up inside. "Thank you. I would love to turn you down, but a shower right about now sounds heavenly."

"So, you have new books in the works?" Lane asks, sounding interested. Or did I imagine the interest?

He thought writing was a bit of a hobby back when we were kids as I was always scribbling in journals. I had few friends outside these two and preferred the imaginative worlds I could create. Today we are older, settled in careers, and I am making a living doing what I love most. Sharing with Lane was important; he understood this evolution.

"I do have a great agent that shopped my last book. I'm with a new publisher for this next trilogy. It is a psychological thriller but with a fair amount of romance." I tell him as I feel my cheeks heat up. At my age, it's silly that just the mention of love or such around Lane elicits this response, but I can't help it.

"Amazing. You think living this far from New York now will impact anything?" He questions.

"Nope, they make these nifty contraptions called computers, and I can email, video conference, and keep in contact," I tease him.

He squints his eyes and glares back at me with a funny grin.

"Well, I, for one, am glad you're home," Kieran interjects. "Unfortunately, I'm going to be heading out for a quick business trip, but Lane is in the house two over."

"Wait. Do you both live on this block? I saw Kieran's massive home from my window but didn't realize yours was that close," I continue. "Why do you need so much space? I didn't think you wanted kids or anything?" I ask, realizing too late how invasive and personal the question was.

"I never said I didn't want kids," Lane grumbles in that voice of his that seems to vibrate my soul. "Just haven't found the right woman yet."

"You have to date to do that," Kieran teases. "I'm on the prowl and hoping I find my soulmate soon. Lane here, though," he thumbs his hand at his friend. "Likes to play hard to get. I promise, should he ever officially make it known that he is open to offers, he will not be lacking in women vying for his attention."

"Our company takes all the time and energy I have available right now," Lane defends. "If the right person was to come along, I'm open to all of that," I notice his gaze lifts to mine, and the air sucks from the room.

I must have gotten knocked harder on the head than I realize because I let myself believe that look was intended for me. I adore children and want a family someday, and my ideal dream is all of that with Lane. This is the second time since my arrival back home that I would swear he is giving off reciprocal vibes. Considering the trauma I've been through and the amazing imagination I am blessed with, I'm certain that can't be the case. Swallowing hard, I try to put on my big girl pants and act like I'm good to banter along with these two.

"Well, I'm sure you'll both impress the right lady with your big houses, amazing company, and all you've accomplished. Now, if you don't mind, I need to earn my keep and try to get some writing done." I turn toward the desk and move my leg to prop up on the little scooter.

"If you need anything, call me," Lane says. "I'll send over the nurse for you to interview—say around two today?"

"Works for me. Safe travels," I tell Kieran. "And remember, downplay the accident if you talk to Mom. The last thing I need is her fussing around here while I'm trying to get strong and meet my deadlines."

"Understood," he said as they both move to exit.

I watch them go, finally taking my first full breath since their entrance. Man, I definitely did not think this through. I hadn't known how close their homes were to mine and that I was going to be seeing both of them all the time. My brother, I'm grateful for, as I've missed him. Lane, though, is wrecking my peace of mind, and continued exposure to the man might be the worst outcome possible. I need to remember to keep it aboveboard and work on burying all those feelings that seem to keep bobbing to the surface. I can do this, and soon he will lose interest and quit coming around as frequently—at least, I can hope.

Chapter 4

Lane

I GLANCE IN THE rearview mirror and plant my palm on my forehead. Nothing says love like throw pillows. That is exactly what the sales lady said when I was checking out. She wasn't wrong, but I sure hope Emma doesn't see these as a declaration or something. When I visited, I noticed that she was still propping her feet up on the scooter. She claims all her belongings are on the way from New York but not due for another ten days. In the meantime, I figure a few throw pillows in the style she liked would serve a dual purpose.

As I take a glance in the same mirror to check that my hair is good and nothing is in between my teeth, I end up growling at the reflection. I don't date or give half a thought to my personal life. These days though, all those years of abstinence focused on my company and the guys I was helping with new leases on life after military service were returning to haunt me. I felt like I was one wrong statement away from declaring myself to Emma, and that kept me on edge.

Maybe continual exposure to her would make me realize that we had grown into different people. After living in the city, she could have become selfish and money motivated. If she was a partier during those years in between or dated a bunch, I might not be as willing to trust her with my heart. I don't know what I am hoping, but I think some light conversation can somehow find something wrong with Emma that will finally make my brain turn this attraction off.

I give a quick rap on the door.

"Come in," she says as I shake my head and enter.

"You do know that anyone could be at the door," I reprimand her as I walk into the office space.

"This is Briar Glen, not the Bronx," she retorts, arching a brow at me.

She is so adorable today I want to grab her and kiss her. Her T-shirt reads: *Don't make me mad; I might plot and get away with your murder in my next book.* The bruises have started to fade, and the shy smile she throws in my direction twists my gut. She has on loose shorts and, with no makeup, looks like an innocent kid. She has not aged, but time has somehow firmed up the edges of her face and turned her hair into a shiny, flowing cascade down her back.

"Love the T-shirt," I utter, as nothing else comes to mind that won't get me reprimanded for saying.

"Thanks. My publisher is always sending me little care packages of swag," she says. "Are those throw pillows?"

Her face is a mix of lust and confusion as she glances at the bags in my hand.

"Yep. I thought your foot"—I point toward where the offending appendage is propped up—"could use some support. Additionally, I know how much you love throw pillows, and something about the lack of them here was making me sad for you."

She gives a cute giggle.

"I do love throw pillows," she says. "Can you show me?"

One by one, I give a dramatic unveiling of the pillows to tiny squeals of happiness. I'm chuckling, she is squeezing her favorite one, and I'm arranging the others on the nearby couch in short order. Pulling up a chair next to her, I settle in after that for a quick visit.

"How are you honestly feeling?" I ask.

"The leg is itchy, my body hates the contortions I need to sit and sleep in to be comfortable, and I would literally give my year's salary for a hot bath," Emma tells me. "Even with all of that, I get to sit here staring out my favorite window and filling pages with inspired writing again," she sighs contentedly. "I didn't have this in the city. The noise and energy always kept me on edge. I'm grateful, even if I have a long road ahead to recovery."

"Why stay in the city if you didn't like it? You know your parents or brother would have welcomed you back with open arms," I question, confused, as this appears to be a long-standing sentiment she has lived with.

"I didn't want to feel like a failure," she confesses. "Kieran, despite trying to hide the truth, was killing it after the military. Mom would gush every time we were on the phone." Emma gave a slight eye roll. "It was hard always living in his shadow, so I wanted to prove I could fulfill my dreams. Besides, New York was the best place for classes, meetups with other authors, and even networking with publishing entities. I think it served a purpose, and I'm grateful for the time there. Right now, though, I want to move on to the next thing in life."

"Well, I, for one, am grateful you're back. You keep things more interesting," I tease her.

"Oh, interesting is a kind way of putting it. I think I kept you and Kieran in stitches most of my childhood with antics," she said as her cheeks reddened. "Do you remember me in the talent show Mom insisted I try to do?"

I laugh out loud as that memory fills my head. Honestly, Emma would do anything then or now to make her parents happy, but baton throwing was absolutely not a talent she should have gone public with. Her mom had been riding her for weeks about attempting to do the show, as she was worried Emma needed to get her nose out of her books. It was a disaster.

"I think that your eye looked worse than it does today when the baton hit you," I tell her, biting hard on my lip to keep from laughing.

"Yep. Just what a sophomore in high school wants is her big brother, home from the Army, watching her get pummeled on stage by a baton," she grimaces. "Then there was the chicken dance video at junior prom, and let's not forget me gracefully falling flat on my face at senior prom."

"Hey, you had a reputation to uphold as the most adorable but slightly awkward high schooler of all time. I give you an A-plus for effort," I tell her as each of those memories plays through my head. "You always got up with a smile on your face and tried again. Is the senior thing the most embarrassing moment of your life? I mean, it was years ago, and I'm sure you have grown in a million ways since then."

"It's not the most embarrassing," she said with the saddest expression as her gaze broke with mine. "That would be throwing myself at the man who thought of me as a sister and making a fool of myself in such a huge way I could not face him for eight years," she whispered under her breath. "I don't think I ever did say sorry about that. I hope it isn't something you'll hold against me."

My breath suspends movement in my lungs as I realize she is talking about me. This is years overdue for us to clear the air, and I know that whatever words I speak in this next sentence can make or break our friendship. I've negotiated a lot of business deals and a few strikes with weapons required—nothing scared me as much as this moment.

"Emma, I never, not for a second, regretted that moment. I think the only thing I regret is not—"

"Hey," Selena, Emma's nurse, walked into the room, breaking the tension and filling the space. "I thought I would stop by and see if you needed anything before the weekend," she says as she glances from one to the other of us. "Did I interrupt something?"

"No. I could really use a little help organizing the room as we discussed," Emma says, turning to me. "Do you mind, Lane?"

"No, I can head out," I tell her, knowing that we need to finish this conversation, but that this isn't the right time or place.

"Thank you for the pillows," she calls out as I head for the door.

"Anytime," I say, turning to her as my eyes alight on her earnest expression.

Something passes between us as I slowly head to exit. This situation is going to need resolution and sooner rather than later. We can't walk around on eggshells forever, or someone in our friend-and-family group will figure it out. I wish I could grab her, kiss her senselessly, and finally put to rest years of unspoken feelings. I'm not sure that would guarantee the results I'm looking for, though, and I'm pretty certain her brother would come for me in a way our friendship could not survive. Better to retreat and regroup than wander in and do something neither of us can come back from, I realize, shutting the door behind me as I escape home.

Chapter 5

Emma

"This is crazy," I mutter as Lane unceremoniously picks me up before I can say another word.

I was trying to make it over to his massive home for dinner, as he requested. Kieran is also there, and it sounds like they will be having a lazy night of grilling. I'm eager to see what the inside of a home completely decorated by a bachelor looks like and get a sneak peek at how nice his home might be. The curiosity since I'd seen him outside of his house was eating me up inside, but the dumb leg situation was making visits quite an undertaking.

The problem started with the watering system and my inability to get my leg wet without ruining the cast. Additionally, there is a sidewalk surrounding the conjoined properties made of stepping stones. They are very nice, chic additions to the lawn ambiance, but not the easiest to ride my scooter over while limping on my good leg. So, here I am, held like a damsel in distress in Lane's arms, being escorted to his front door.

I keep my gaze from him, though his breath on the back of my neck is causing goosebumps over every square inch of my flesh. I will admit that in some of my naughtier journal entries, I had penned something like this, but it ended with declarations of love that I was pretty certain would not be happening this evening, especially not with my brother waiting for us at the front door.

"Wow, you arrive in style, princess," Kieran scoffs as Lane lowers me to the ground inside the foyer.

On the ceiling there are open beams exposed, creating a warm, cozy feel despite the obvious massive size of the home. Each piece is perfectly positioned, with sofas facing the huge fireplace, beckoning for cozy nights in winter. The kitchen off to the right, even from a distance, is clearly amazing and a cook's dream. I glance around and have to wonder at all the sweet pictures and little touches that I could add to make the magnificent space nearly my ideal living environment if I were able to decorate a home from scratch.

"Did you hire someone to do this for you?" I ask Lane, confused.

"Nah, my man said he had a vision for his home," Kieran slapped his best friend on the back. "This man poured over magazines and online catalogs, and he made me go with him to a thousand different markets to find every piece. I took the easy route and found someone named Esme, who did my entire house in about a third of the time it took Lane."

"I just wanted it to be all mine," Lane says as he turns to me. "I think a home needs to be comfortable and an extension of the people living in it. Whether a one-room studio or a mansion."

"I agree," I tell him. "Though, it could use a few throw pillows," I tease based on the addition to my own space the man made a few days before.

"No throw pillows," Kieran states. "I swear that I was finding those little fluffy squares in the attic, your room, and even in my boxes Mom packed up after I left home and enlisted."

"Good. I like to make sure you remember me," I tell him. "I think you did a wonderful job, and the home is beautiful." I awkwardly try to turn as best as I can to take it all in.

"Thanks. I'm pretty proud of it," Lane returns. "You hungry?" he adds, holding out his hand. "We can go sit out back as the weather is nearly perfect outside."

"Starving. I sat and stared at a blank screen all day, willing the words to come," I mutter.

"Writer's block?" Kieran asked. "Does that happen often?"

"No, honestly, I'm super blessed to write what I love, so it normally flows easily. This story I got about halfway through, and then the struggle became real," I say. "I have a deadline to hit, so I need to get out of this state. You know I love my alone time, but man, with my body healing and no ability to move around without a big production, I find my concentration is suffering. I know I'll kick back into gear soon enough," I tell him, adding silently to myself that this is the hope, but I'm not overly confident.

"Well, if you need comedy inspiration, we are the go-to team," Kieran replied. "If it is romance inspiration, I'm going to have to be the one to help," he said as Lane went to put a plate of burgers on the grill. "My man is married to his job, and you should see the women trying to get him to take notice. I think that we might need to have Lane examined for a physical problem."

"Nothing wrong with me," he grumbles as Kieran laughs loudly. "I just like to be a bit more discerning than you are," he turns to my brother.

"You date a lot?" I ask, curious now.

Kieran has had girlfriends in the past but no relationship of any merit that made it more than a few outings. I always wonder about that, as I think my brother is incredible, though I might be biased as his baby sister. He had a lot of friends that were girls, though none as close as I was with Lane back in the day, despite huge age gaps. My mother also brought up the lack of love in Kieran's life.

"Hey, I like to have a good time, but you know that I subscribe to the lifetime commitment theory of relationships. I never take them too seriously, as I'm not someone that wants to date for the sake of having someone around. Like Mom and Dad, I believe that when my soul mate comes along, I will know it," Kieran said. "No need to hurry her along, as I love the job, my service, and the guys I get to spend time helping when they get back from a tour of duty. I'm not in a rush to settle down at this stage of my life."

"How many veterans have you helped so far?"

"Hundreds," Lane said. "We hire a bunch of them as testers, put some through coding school to work for us, and others work in sales."

"We work with them through the nonprofit to help with mental health and other needs," Kieran adds.

"I think that a lot of what they get from our company is the camaraderie and the ability to be around others that understand what they have been through," he confirms.

"That is astounding. I guess you are doing all right for yourself, even single," I tell Kieran.

"Yeah, but I still hope I find my dream partner." He sighs, taking a swig of his soda as my eyes travel to Lane.

I'm shocked to find the latter's eyes on me. With all this talk of soul mates, I have to wonder what his feelings are. Is he truly not dating because he doesn't see a family in his future? He himself told me that kids and the like are something he would consider, so that makes no sense. He is successful, has money, and is handsome as sin—so what is it? I have to wonder.

"So, what about you?" Kieran asks. "Anyone special in New York?"

I laugh, actually more like a snort. The thought of dating was not one that I had entertained.

"I'm a slightly overweight, petite, introvert that prefers made-up boyfriends to real ones," I tell him. "No one special."

"Curvy," Lane says under his breath. "You aren't overweight, and real men don't like stickpins. We like curvy."

As I sit there dumbfounded, Kieran looks at his friend with the funniest expression. I can tell from the blush now staining Lane's cheeks he didn't intend to say that outloud, or maybe how it came out sounding. I feel my breath catch and my heart skip a beat, as that may be the sweetest thing any man has ever said to me.

"What? I don't like people putting themselves down," he defends, putting his attention back on the burgers as Kieran looks at me and then his friend. There is a curious expression on his face, but I'm pretty certain it is time to change the topic, as the air is getting a little stifling.

"So, did Mom call you about Thanksgiving?"

That did the trick, as Kieran laughs.

"Yes, four months from now, and she already needs us to commit to a plan," he said, launching into his thoughts on us traveling this year.

Three and a half hours later, Kieran walks me to my door. I am full, happy, and had the best evening.

Trying to make my way through the hallway to bed, I feel this crazy energy flowing as inspiration hits. I know exactly how the hero in this book needs to act, and I have a great idea for the next scene I had been stuck on earlier.

Hobbling to the desk, I sit down, adjust my leg onto a throw pillow, and go to town. The words flow from my fingertips as the hero takes shape, and the story starts to come to life with each word I type.

Chapter 6

Lane

I FINISH MAKING THE frittata and add some fruit to the tray I am compiling. I have been up for two hours and have already gotten in a workout, so the endorphins are buzzing and making me excited for the day ahead. After the visit the night before, I am feeling on top of the world and want to make sure Emma gets her day off to a fabulous start. I know she's been struggling with the pain, being cooped up during the day, and having some writer's block to make things worse. I figure some home-cooked food to start the day might be the kick in the backside she needs to have a wonderful day.

I head across the yard and find myself moving quickly as it dawns on me that I completely forgot how exposed to Kieran's house I was on the path to Emma. When building our homes on the block, we strategically placed everything for maximum sun and hosting capabilities while maintaining the privacy of Kieran's family home. I don't think my sneaking in to see Emma, for fear of her brother's strong opinions, was properly considered during the planning phase of our homes. I sure hope that doesn't come back to bite me now.

I walk around the corner and hold my breath. The last time the anticipation of being caught by a disapproving figure came into play was ages ago. In high school, Kieran and I snuck out to go to a concert that ended up being terrible. Of course, in the end, we got caught and a grounding from the other's presence was the punishment. Even if Kieran finds out that I am sneaking about, I doubt that he will do anything drastic, but that is because I have the perfect cover. He doesn't need to know it is my heart driving me and not the best intentions of a friend helping one on the road to recovery.

"It's me," I announce, working to balance the tray and open the door.

"I'm in the office," Emma's voice calls out, and I follow it.

"Good morning." I smile at her, and the returning display has my stomach knotting and my insides turning to warm liquid.

"Morning. You did not cook me breakfast!" she exclaims, taking in the tray.

"Heavy workout on my side, so I just doubled what I would eat. I figure you are healing and need just about the same proteins," I offer, sitting the tray on the pin-neat desk. "Can we eat in here?"

She looks the items over with a chuckle. "Even down to the fork, you thought of everything. Sure. Perfect timing, as I can use a break," she finishes, turning the laptop cover down.

"You writing this early?" I ask, intrigued, as I thought she was at an impasse.

"I came home last night inspired, and the storyline just took fire in my belly," she reports, with a shake of her head. "I have gotten in chapters since I left you, and just a short cat nap on the couch there." She inclined her hand to the furniture directly behind me.

"I thought that was the same outfit from last night, but I didn't want to say anything." I chuckle. "I'm glad the writer's block seems to have lifted."

"Me too," she says.

As we eat we chat more about the writing, her plans for the day, and even some ideas for rehabbing the house when she feels better. It is a great start to the day, but I don't have time to dawdle, considering I have a meeting in just a few minutes over at Kieran's home office space.

"I need to head out," I say as I glance at my watch nervously. "Kieran can be a bit over the top when anyone is late to one of his meetings."

"I love that about him. If you're on time, that is ten minutes late by his definition," Emma tells me.

"Oh, I know. You remember I was chronically late in high school, and your brother is the number one reason I broke out of that habit," I tell her with a scared expression. "Will Selena be coming by today?"

"Yep. I get a shower and hopefully another inspirational tidal wave, along with some physical therapy movements she thought might help with the cramping during the day."

"Awesome. Well, I'm sure we can connect later, then," I tell her, lingering a moment longer. The desire to hug her or even kiss those supple lips is nearly overwhelming to my common sense. I clear my throat, "I should . . ." I thumb my finger over my shoulder. "See ya."

"Have a good day," she calls out to my back as I break into a goofy grin.

If I thought I was feeling good with some heavy cardio under my belt, breakfast with Emma just topped my tank off. It was going to be a phenomenal day, and I don't think anything will get to me now.

I place the empty tray right inside Kieran's door and head for his office.

"Morning," I call out as he pivots to me with the angriest of expressions I've ever seen from my best friend, directed toward me. "What did I do?"

"Did you have breakfast with Emma? Like make her breakfast in bed, on that fancy little tray you were trying to hide as you crossed the yard a little while ago," he demands. "I couldn't believe my eyes, but I didn't want to upset her or walk in on something." He shudders violently.

"*No.* I mean, yes, I made her breakfast because she can't walk," I defend myself.

"She does have a caretaker for that." Kieran was still looking at me like I was a bug he intended to squash.

"Kieran, she can't walk, I did a workout, and then made breakfast. I figured I could double everything up and take it over to her. For goodness' sake, I wouldn't march across the lawn in front of you and then ravage your sister," I said, as if that thought disgusted me.

What kind of friend does he think I am? I might be in love with Emma, but I would never disrespect him in that manner.

"Really?"

"Yes. Besides, your sister is in a cast and can barely get around—how active do you think she could be first thing in the morning," I said, then planted a palm on my forehead at how terrible that sounded.

"Okay, maybe we quit talking words like 'ravaging' and other stuff," he said, holding up his hands in surrender. "I appreciate you making sure my sister eats, but maybe let's hold the breakfast in bed bit for now."

"She was up in the office writing," I said, thinking that might make him feel better.

"Really?"

"Yeah, napped there overnight, as she said the writing was finally coming through," I tell him, noticing his expression soften.

"That is good news," he concedes. "I'm sorry; I can't tell you the terrible thoughts that ran through my head when I saw you crossing the lawn."

"Oh, I think you made yourself plenty clear on what thoughts you were having," I drolly retort.

"Can we get ready for this call now?" he says, making an effort to turn the tide of the conversation.

"Please," I say, moving to the chair opposite his desk, happy to focus on anything but the topic of Emma.

This is bad. I cannot continue like this without Kieran, Emma, or both of them figuring out my feelings. Maybe it was time to rip the Band-Aid off and talk to Emma. If she felt anywhere near the same, it might be worth risking sitting Kieran down to see about a future plan for them all. If she didn't, why burn unnecessary bridges? I need to get on this call now, but that was definitely a problem I was going to address before long, and I sure was praying things went in the direction I hoped for. My single state of denial about my emotions and relationship status could soon be a thing of the past and the happiest of futures mine for the taking.

Chapter 7

Emma

"I'm thrilled you loved the new chapters. I am playing with the characters more," I tell my editor, Regina Olstein. "I am finding the new love narratives interactions richer and deepening the story and mystery. I hope you liked how I was weaving that together."

"It was fantastic, and the depth of the story, in general, is perfect," she gushes as we finish the conversation regarding the new deliverables I sent her last night. I'm ready to conquer this book and get it in for its first full draft. I don't think I've ever done this level of writing so quickly, and it might be my best work yet.

I'm watching the screen but notice that in the right-hand corner, where my notifications scroll, a new one is reflected to me. I notice the headline regarding BattleBorn Tech, my brother and Lane's company.

That, of course, immediately grabs my attention away from the meeting.

I have been researching Kieran and Lane's company over the last few days. Call me curious, but everything I could find indicates they are a cutting-edge, one-to-follow tech company. Additionally, the amount of profits dedicated to helping veterans thrive is a big point in their favor, according to numerous sites I found.

"Please let me know when you have the last portion done. I will get it edited and back ASAP," Regina says as she readies to end the call.

"Will do," I tell her absently and disconnect as I simultaneously hit the notification to read the information.

My breath is shallow, and my brain is spinning by the end of it. I don't understand why they tried to downplay the success of their company. Billionaires is what the article says, as I stare out the windows at the massive homes in my line of sight. I knew they were doing well, no matter the untruths they had spoken. Sure, they gave a lot of credit to their team, some lucky breaks, and their experience in the military. Nothing that indicated their statuses as billionaires, though.

"You okay?" Kieran asks as I jolt in my seat.

"You scared me," I tell him.

"You look pale." Kieran briskly walks in my direction. "Has Selena checked on you today?"

"Yes," I tell him, flipping the laptop around so that he can see the screen. "Really? You lied to me."

"No, we simply didn't give the full story," he says and sighs, falling into the guest chair opposite my desk. "Also, we individually are not of billionaire status. The business is valued in that neighborhood, but we don't need that sort of money. The houses paid off, a car to drive, and all the incredible amenities we already have is enough. Reinvesting as much as possible toward others is vital to what we do."

"Why not tell me all of this before?" I demand, still not understanding why he wouldn't give me some context of his wealth. "You never had to give me a dollar amount or anything but you always said you were doing all right and then changed the subject from the company when we were together. Why?"

He bows his head, exhaling.

"The truth?" he asks with the most serious expression. I feel beads of sweat form down my back, and goosebumps invade every inch of my skin.

"Yes, please," I request.

"I love you and didn't want to make you feel less than. I always wanted to be in the military, and this was a side hustle that, crazily, blew up. You were born to be a writer, but your path to success was a bit trickier. I didn't want to make you feel like I was somehow boasting when you struggled. Lane and I agreed to tell you what was necessary to not be a lie, as you didn't come here for years—so the full extent of our success was pretty easy to hide when you were a distance away."

"I see," I mumble. "Lane agreed to this lie."

"Emma," Kieran replies softly. "It was truly not a lie but rather just a slight softening of the details related to our finances only. You can't tell me that you wouldn't have been upset that we just lucked into such a huge windfall with these games of ours when you were struggling to make ends meet."

"I wasn't struggling these last few years. Sure, writing is a bit of a roller coaster when it comes to payments. I get advances and then nothing until a book is published, but the checks got bigger with the successes. Sure, I will never be a billionaire, but I'm happy with what I have. I wish you didn't feel the need to lie to protect me, but I guess there is nothing that can be done about that."

"So, we are good?"

"Sure," I tell him, but my heart is breaking. If I thought I was out of Lane's league before, this sure seals the deal. "You know, they call the two of you the most eligible bachelors in our state."

"That is just something they say to sell papers." Kieran rolls his eyes. "I have no desire to have hordes of women chasing me for the money. I work hard for everything and have no intention to kick back and take it easy anytime soon. You should know that we didn't participate in the writing of that article, so take it all with a grain of salt."

"Hmmm," was all I could manage.

While Kieran might not be using his status to find women, that didn't mean that someone wouldn't come knocking. I have to be realistic that a petite, curvy little sister of his best friend would not draw Lane's attention over the type of women that normally adorn men's arms with their resources. It is just a fact, and nothing I can do anything about—so no use crying over spilled milk. Some things are not meant to be, and I can't change them simply by wishing they are different.

Chapter 8

Lane

"HOW IS EMMA?" I ask as I notice that Kieran, who went to extend a dinner invite, returns with his head down. My instincts home in super quickly as I worry that maybe something is wrong with her. For the longest time, Kieran doesn't say a word.

"She knows," he whispers ominously as my heart squeezes painfully. "That journalist that you tried to dissuade from writing the fluff piece on us didn't honor her agreement," he mutters, moving to the dual-screened computer he uses in this lab and typing something in. When he backs away, I see the splashy headline.

"Great! Just what we need. You know the crazies are sure to come out of the woodwork," I spit out, shaking my head. "So, Emma, I guess, did not take it well?"

"She thinks that we didn't tell her, as we were ashamed or maybe pitying her." He shrugged. "I'm sorry; I know she is my sister, but she's also a woman. I don't understand the logic. She just asked for a little space."

"How much space does she need? So we have a few more resources than we let on; that shouldn't be a problem that has her turning her back on us," I tell him, confusion heavy in my mind.

"You wouldn't think so, but she isn't coming to dinner. You can be my guest and try to talk reason into her yourself," Kieran finishes with a big dramatic wave toward the door.

"Fine. I just finished that code and need you to test it anyway," I tell him, getting out of the seat. "I will be right back."

"Good luck," he mumbles as I race to Emma's.

I can't allow her to stop the momentum we are on. Things are great. Well, maybe not that great, as she does have a badly broken leg and can't get around on her own. Overall, she is writing, getting more mobile the closer we get to the day of the cast removal, and to be honest, things with the three of us are better than ever. One little article simply cannot tear that apart—I won't allow it.

"I'm here," I call out, continuing into the main area of the house and into her den.

"I'm not up to guests," Emma says, not meeting my eyes.

"Well, I hear that you read something about me and your brother. I think we should discuss it," I tell her, waiting for some reaction as she types away on the computer, ignoring me.

"Emma, you can't expect to just tune me out and go about your business."

"Why not? You made decisions about what you should tell me over the years. Oh, and I'm pretty certain you both are probably laughing at me behind my back. *'Oh, poor Emma, if only she had as much as we do, we must protect her.'* Well, I'm doing just fine for myself, and I'm not embarrassed by my success. I do what I enjoy, I provide a good living for myself, and I'm happy," she said, though the tone in which she barks that last remark makes it appear inaccurate.

"Emma," I say softly. "We should have told you, as I know it did come up, and there were efforts made to downplay our success. Maybe we did it for the wrong reasons, but now you know. This changes nothing between us, and I need you to know that not everything people print about us is always accurate."

She laughs. "Right, it's just creative fiction, and you are only millionaires. You don't have women admirers and aren't the most eligible bachelors in the state?"

"This is your latest chapter," I say, looking at the marked-up pages on the side of her desk.

"Yes."

I pick it up, and notice Emma struggle to reach for me as I start to read out loud:

His blue eyes meet mine across the blazing fire. He has tormented my dreams for years, and now we are separated by a heat more intense than the one burning in my nether regions. I thought I loved a man in uniform, but I would prefer a glimpse of that chest out of the firefighter uniform stretched over his muscles. He might be the best friend to my brother—

"What in the world is that?" Kieran's voice shouts as I drop the papers all over the floor.

I had not heard Kieran enter the room and had no idea he might overhear me reading the clip. As I turn to Emma, she looks just as shocked by his sudden appearance. I feel like I have been caught reading Emma's diary, and my fingers are not as nimble as they should be as I attempt to retrieve the papers.

"I was just trying to prove that anyone can write fiction, and even journalists sometimes exaggerate," I defend my actions.

"I tried to get him to stop," Emma groans as I turn to see her lay her head in her hands.

"Is that your latest book?" Kieran demands as I roll my eyes toward the ceiling. "Because that sounds a lot like a good description of Lane here. Is it?"

The question hangs in the room, as not a sound is made. The silence becomes deafening and all I hear is my heart pounding.

Finally, she picks her head up and looks right at me.

"He was the inspiration for the kind of man the heroine of my story loves," she says, "but obviously, it's just fiction as he's way out of my league no matter what he claims the writer of that article got wrong. He can have any woman he wants, so don't worry—inspiration is all it will ever be," she says as she juts her chin out a bit more. "I hope you both find someone that loves you for you, and not just your bank balances."

"Emma," I say softly.

"Listen," Kieran starts.

"I need you both to go," Emma demands.

No one moves.

"Now. I have writing to do, if you don't mind," she says, turning to start clicking out keys on the laptop again.

I turn to Kieran, but he has already started to walk away. As I see him retreat, I turn one last time to see that she is fully engrossed in her work. I have no choice but to take a knee in this battle and surrender. Whatever had been blossoming to life here between us appears to have died with a single article. I know that when Emma puts her mind to something, changing it rarely happens.

I turn, shoulders slumping, and hope that, given time to process, Emma will come around. I don't care what it takes; I will find a way to get her to fully understand how wrong she is. Emma is the only woman in my league with all the attributes I care about, and based on that clip from her book, hope is alive and well that I can win her over. I'll give her time to reflect, and then I'm going to wage a campaign to take her heart—and this time, never let her out of my sight again.

Chapter 9

Emma

I WISH, WITH EVERY fiber of my being, that I could leave my hometown and never face the two most influential men in my life again. I had thought we were the three musketeers and back together after all this time. What a fool I had been, and if not for this leg limiting my mobility, I would have made good on a retreat despite how lonely my existence without them always was.

It has been four days, and I've started to pay Selena's salary myself as of seventy-two hours ago. I realized that her being fully under my payroll allowed me to dictate her activities, including keeping two pesky billionaires away from my front door. The woman had not been dealing with grumpy, hurting, and injured patients all these years without growing some thick skin. I could hear Lane and Kieran when they stopped by daily, but thus far, she held them off from entering. I was not budging as of yet.

The cell phone on my desk vibrates in circles as I glance at the caller ID. It is my mother, and for the span of a heartbeat, I consider not answering. I don't know if she is going to plead my brother's case, but I need everyone to leave me in peace for a little while longer so I can work through my feelings. I, of course, am going to continue a relationship with my brother, despite my current misgivings. There will be new boundaries about the exclusion of information or outright lies when I talk to him, but that isn't something I don't think we can overcome. The bigger issue is Lane.

The man is seriously making me start to think about a relationship. I could see those sparks in his eyes, and I convinced myself that they were interests that mirrored my own. I know now that simply cannot be the case. He chose not to see me for years; he has money to attract any woman he wants and an amazing career that makes him even more respected. The man is smoking hot; he looks like a ten in uniform and, honestly, is too nice to me. I need the space to rid my heart of the yearnings for him, as the anger I feel is already starting to fade. Avoiding my mother is not going to accomplish anything but add fuel to the fire of this showdown.

"Hey, Mom," I answer, glancing at the clock on my computer. "I have a reading at the library in an hour, and based on how fast I move, I need to leave soon."

"Are you walking?"

"I'm scooting," I tell her. "The weather is perfect here, and I'm looking forward to the exercise."

"I think maybe I do need to make the trip to stay with you." She sounds worried.

I love my mother more than anything, but having her always underfoot like a mother hen would be a fate worse than death, in my opinion. She would make me eat all healthy food when I preferred the occasional brownie or salty snack. I consider the doctor's advice in my healing process, and he said indulging in moderation was okay. Of course, my definition and my mother's definition wouldn't match. Also, she would want to broker a peace treaty with my brother and Lane.

I could already hear her now asking about how we felt. Yuck, and no, thank you. I am mad, hurt, and not needing my mommy around to baby me. This will pass, and life always comes full circle. Just give me time, I wanted to shout at everyone.

"Mom, we discussed this, and I don't need a mother babysitter," I tell her firmly. "I'm doing rehab, have a caretaker on hand for anything I need, and besides, I have a ton of writing to get through each day. You would want to talk about feelings, make me take it easy, and all the other things I do love about you—just not when I'm on a deadline."

"How is the new book coming?" She took the bait, switching the conversation in a new direction.

"Great. I should be hitting the end here in the next day or so. I was worried after the accident that I wouldn't get over the writer's block—and then it just started to flow," I tell her.

"You know I need to read a copy," she says, as my heart constricts.

I didn't know that my mother wanted to read anything. She is not a reader by nature, and this is the first time she had made such a request. In all the years that I have been writing, I truly can't recall her picking up one of my stories. Now, based on the character inspiration being Lane in this latest endeavor, I want to squash that request of hers out of hand. Doing that abruptly might raise some flags, especially if Kieran is the cause behind her offer.

"Mom, you don't read a lot. I didn't know you would want to read anything of mine," I tell her.

"Your brother might not be the only one in the family keeping secrets," she said ominously.

My heart rate picks up exponentially, and worry twists my insides. What did she mean by that? I knew Kieran's secrets, and I pray no one knows mine—so that only left her with something to hide.

"What secrets?" I ask cautiously.

"I've read everything you've ever published. I even joined a book club that read your last novel. It was delightful talking to so many people that enjoyed a book you wrote," she adds enthusiastically.

"Oh man, I had no idea." I utter a slight groan. "When did we all start keeping secrets from each other in this family?"

"Well, you at fourteen when you fell for Lane and your brother pretty much since puberty when I found those magazines under his bed," she said.

I, of course, am not breathing at this point. Did she tell me she knew about Lane? What in the world—how?

"Mom, about Lane."

"If you try to tell me that you don't love that man, I will call your bluff. Listen, I've never told your brother, but he is worried sick that he broke your relationship with the secrets he's been keeping. I don't want to disillusion him, but I would bet that this latest revelation about Lane's financial position has made you feel more than ever you are not good enough for him. Let me tell you, he would be lucky to have you. I need you to think long and hard about continuing to cold-shoulder those two men that love you over one silly little news article written by a woman trying to make a name for herself. Oh, and then please, for the love of all that is good, marry Lane and give me some grandbabies," she demands.

I nearly choke on that request. Honestly, my well-ordered, boring life has taken a turn into a dramedy, and I'm not sure how to make it stop!

"I have to go, Mom," I tell her. "I need to head out to make it on time for the reading. Please, I can't talk about this now, but I'll call so we can clear the air soon," I offer as the only thing I can at the moment in this state of mind.

"I love you and understand. You aren't getting any younger, though, so don't hold out much longer," she responds.

"I love you too." I finish with her and slide my finger over the cell phone screen to disconnect.

"You ready?" Selena asks before I can even catch my breath.

"I guess so," I reply as I clumsily attempt to get to my feet.

She moves forward to lend an arm, but I wave her away. I need to feel independent just for a moment. The constant push of everyone else's needs on me along with the limitations of my injury are seriously impacting my mental health.

"I have to do this," I tell her, worried that I might hurt her feelings.

"I will spot you and lend help only if you look as if you're going to fall," she offers back, and I give a nod of agreement.

I line up the scooter, take the messenger bag with my marked-up book that I will be reading from, along with extra pens if anyone wants a signature. Flinging the strap over my head, I center myself and take off for the front door.

It's a slow journey, but I make it with only needing Selena to help me twice to regain my balance for curbs. I don't think I will be running any marathons in the near future, but I didn't fall on my face, so I will celebrate any victories I get.

I don't recognize the librarian who comes over with all the information Regina sent her. Soon I'm moving slowly to the front of a good-sized audience. I'm pleasantly surprised that the room is more full than many of my readings in New York. I start to worry that they have me confused with another author just as the librarian launches into introductions.

"Thank you," I say as the introduction is over, and I'm allowed to lean into my presentation. "I know that I write novels that are in a variety of genres, but my favorite to write are psychological thrillers. I love the good mind-bending elements of psychological thrillers, the deep mystery, and well-developed characters. I would love to read from one of my last books for everyone today and then a secret excerpt or two from a book to be released early next year."

A hand goes up.

"Yes?"

"Will you do autographs?"

"At the end," I agree, as the girl claps like a giddy teenager, though I would put her age closer to mine.

The audience is fully engrossed as I get through the first two pages. There are good questions, and it is obvious many of them are fans as they reference other works of mine. The time passes surprisingly quickly as

I proudly talk about the career I am so happy to have been successful in achieving.

A motion in the corner of my eye draws my attention. Lane in full fireman regalia stands there, hip popped out against a shelf, just listening to my reading. His gaze is hooded, and that handsome face is brooding today. He hasn't shaved in at least a day, and man, if that shadow doesn't just pump his hotness to a twenty on a scale often. I wish I was immune to his charms, but all I can do is look away.

"Are there any other questions?"

I notice Lane raises his hand.

I glance around, and as I don't see anyone else with their hand up, I finish the meeting.

"I will sign autographs for anyone who would like one," I announce, trying to keep my eyes off of Lane.

My mind returns to my mother's comments about how she must have known I adored this man since we were children. Does he know about these feelings of mine? Does he enjoy making a mockery of me and feeding his ego? Is he here just because of the falling out with my brother? An even bigger question occurs—why is he still volunteering as a firefighter for Glen Briar?

That seems dangerous for a man so vital to a bigger organization. I hadn't considered this before, but as he makes his way to me, I wonder at his tenacity. He waits at the back of the line, allowing everyone to pass him before finally bringing a book to me for my signature.

"Lane, how would you like me to sign your book?"

"Surprise me," he replies.

I stumble as my brain goes blank. The niceties I would normally inscribe all seem too personal, and in the end, I swipe my autograph across the page.

"Why do you still volunteer as a firefighter?" I ask the question forefront in my mind.

"Because deep down, I'm still the boy that loves a good adrenaline rush, helping my community, and always doing whatever I can for our hometown." He sighs. "Really, nothing has changed from the dreams we used to chat about late at night. I am still Lane, just with bigger toys," he finishes with a deep rumble of a laugh.

I find my eyes traveling the length of him.

Our eyes lock for the longest moment as the world fades away around us.

"I think that is pretty admirable, and I'm sure everyone around here admires you for your sacrifices," I tell him. "Thank you for coming out to support me."

"Always," he says as someone taps my arm.

I go to close out the evening, but I can feel his eyes on me.

"You good, boss?" Selena asks.

"I need you to distract him as I'm getting out of here," I tell her as I slightly look over my shoulder to confirm Lane is still focused on me.

"I was born for this," she tells me as I square my shoulders and make ready for a hasty retreat back to the safety of my home.

Chapter 10

Lane

EMMA IS SO STUBBORN; I swear she is going to be the death of me. The woman read passages tonight before she saw me standing in the audience that I would swear describe me to a T. I couldn't believe after the three of us had dinner that night and inspiration struck, that meant she was all but writing me into her book. At least she made me the main character and didn't kill me off in some disgusting manner—though after this last week, I wasn't going to hold my breath for my continued health in the rest of the book.

"Hey, you know you shouldn't be stalking her, right?" Selena scolds, walking right up to me as I attempt to keep Emma in my line of sight.

We need to talk tonight! This cat-and-mouse game and silence from her are driving Kieran and me up a wall. I think we need to have a heart-to-heart and figure out a way forward. I wasn't going to leave her in peace until I said my piece.

"Maybe get her to quit acting like some wronged party. We didn't do anything to hurt her," I argue.

I can tell from the way Selena's shoulders sag she can see my side of things. I also realize that with her being paid to protect and care for Emma during this time of healing, she is torn. This sweet soul wants to do what is best and has no dog in this fight other than to make certain Emma is safe.

"She knows that. I believe she has a bruised ego, and in time things will go back to how they once were. Until then, I am paid to keep her happy and on the path to a full recovery, so could you just leave," she told me.

"Traitor. You were hired by me, or did you forget that?"

"I did not, but I figure Kieran and you always have each other's backs, and Emma just needed a friend here," Selena responds.

"Fair enough," I look around and notice that Emma is nowhere in sight.

My squinted eyes turn to Selena, and I know she was sent as a decoy. Emma might think that she has the upper hand, but the woman can barely move, and today that was going to even the odds in my favor. I bound around Selena before the woman even knows what is happening and leave the library. Glancing up and down the sidewalk, I'm rewarded with a view of Emma's retreating back, making the fastest getaway a handicapped person probably can—it is a bit impressive if I'm being honest.

I jog forward as several people greet me. I notice Emma turn around to see me hot on her trail, and then somehow, she manages to pick up the pace. The woman is going to break her neck next, as the streets are uneven, the pavement caved in several places she is navigating near, and there is traffic out—granted, not as much as she is used to in New York, but for a one-legged pedestrian, it is an effective death trap without proper concentration.

Part of me worries that I should let her go and not continue to pursue her in case she could get hurt. I would never be able to forgive myself if she was seriously injured, but when she finally clears all of downtown for the much smoother sidewalks leading to our neighborhood, I give proper chase and jump in front of her.

"Move aside," Emma says indignantly. "I've asked you and my brother to leave me be for a little while. I need some time; why is that so hard to understand?"

Tears well up in her eyes as she pleads with me, nearly undoing my resolve. I know that I must forge on in my intent to win her back to my side. I cannot keep up trying to work and go about my day when all I want to do is throw myself on my sword and beg for any punishment if only it means she will allow me back into her presence. It's so corny, but I was accustomed to having her around, and this silent treatment and exile are making me unbearable to be around.

"Because I finally have you back with me, and knowing you're so close, yet so far away, is driving me mad," I confess. I'm tired of trying to dance around the main issue. Yes, she and Kieran have things to work out, and I'm here to help them in any way needed. Right this second, though, I need her to give me a break and start seeing me again regularly, or I might lose my mind.

"Lane, I understand why you all tried to spare my feelings. I've come to understand and accept it. I promise we will be best buds—" I cut her off by moving close and bending to take her lips with mine.

The sweet and tangy taste of her lips short circuits my entire body. I swear I hear birds singing, fireworks fill my brain, and my heart sighs. She is so short next to me that I feel protective as I hold her waist to ensure she won't fall. For several heartbeats, she doesn't move a muscle and then she pulls back enough to stare up into my eyes.

"That is a new way to silence me," she states.

"Yep. I've dreamed of doing that since the night I turned you away," I admit.

"What?" she utters under her breath as the shock is evident in her eyes.

"I have loved you for so long. No one could eclipse the hold you had on my heart. It didn't matter if I traveled continents with the military or made money playing video games; you were always the motivation in my mind. I love your smile, your laugh, your dedication to your writing, your love of family, and most of all, I love you," I tell her, pouring all the feelings I've bottled up for years into the speech. "I shouldn't have lied or allowed Kieran to hide things from you. I honestly knew you wouldn't like it, but—"I stop, realizing that I had no excuse that could rationalize it. If I want this to end with her kissing me back, I need to own my mistakes.

"I was wrong. I promise never to shortchange you or hide anything from you again."

"Lane. We are in very different places in our life," she says as I feel her pull back from me a bit more. "I think we can be friends, but more than that is just not possible."

"Okay," I say, trying to hold the tears at bay. "Just say the words to me, and I will never bring this up again," I tell her as she looks at me with a quizzical expression.

"Fine. Say what words?" she asks.

"Tell me you don't love me. You say that, looking into my eyes, and this is the last time I ever bring this up. If you love me, however, maybe kiss me back and tell me you will never go another day without me by your side."

She doesn't speak for what seems like an eternity. I watch a battle of emotions wage over her expressive face as she bites her lower lip before she turns up to look me in the eyes. I wish I could read her mind as my entire future hangs on whatever comes out of her mouth next. I wish I knew, beyond all doubts, going into this showdown, how it would end. Even if she loved me once, I might have ruined it by not trusting her enough with my secrets and the full honesty she deserved. My breath suspends as I wait for the judgment call that will change my life forever, for better or worse—only she knew.

"I-I-" she stutters, then throws her arms around my neck with an exasperated sigh. "Screw it. You know I love you, and if you're willing to saddle yourself with me, I'll never spend another day—"

I kiss her right there in the middle of the street. I don't know how many people gossip about us or what reaches her brother. I already asked him and her parents for permission earlier today to make a play for her, and I plan to put a ring on her hand the second I get the chance.

"I love you," I whisper into her ear. It is amazing to be able to say those words out loud.

Every thought I had over the years of how our coming together would transpire, this was not it. I nearly lost her, and had she not been injured, she might have given me a better chase. I am never going to make that mistake again, and every day I will put her best interests first as long as she gives me the chance to love her with every fiber of my being.

"And I love you," she sighs as I kiss her once more for good measure. Horns honk all around us and our little town gets a happily ever after they will be talking about for years to come.

THE END

I hope you fell in love with Lane and Emma as much as I did. This was the first story I wrote and I completely adore them!

Don't miss the rest of the Briar Glen Romantic Comedies. You can find all three standalone clean romance stories on Amazon.

Lane & Emma's Story: Rescued by my Brother's Best Friend

Kieran & Maya's Story: Kissing my Best Friend's Brother

Zander & Paige's Story: Second Chance with my Firefighter Best Friend

If you loved Lane & Emma's story then you'll definitely want to read about Kieran & Maya in Kissing my Best Friend's Brother. It's Kieran's turn to fall in love and he's met his match in this enemies to lovers romantic comedy.

(Click here to get Kissing my Best Friend's Brother)

Read chapter one on the very next page!

Sneak Peek

Kissing my Best Friend's Brother

A burning piñata, a smoldering bush, and an unexpected blast from the past.

Kieran:

As a volunteer firefighter, people are usually happy to see me.

My sister's best friend didn't get that memo.

Bright-eyed Maya Glenn is not the awkward girl I remember.

My high school crush is now a beautiful woman, glowering at me like I'm public enemy number one.

Maya:

Kieran Mitchell is the billionaire CEO of Briar Glen's biggest company, and he needs an event planner.

I want it to be me.

But years ago, he stole my heart and my brother. My family may never forgive me for working with him.

Spending time with him, old feelings resurface. Now, he's taking up more of my thoughts than I'm willing to admit.

A re-ignited spark. Our sordid past. I need to stay away, but all I can think about is kissing my best friend's brother.

(Click here to get Kissing my Best Friend's Brother)

Chapter One
Kieran

"Is that a piñata on fire?" Lane asks as we arrive at the scene of the call we had been dispatched to less than four minutes ago.

There is chaos as one of the engines starts toward the smoldering bushes with a grill sticking out of them. Our three-man team heads for the crackling piñata to put it out.

"Your dad pushed mine," one boy says, shoving another kid as hard as possible.

"He was saying that my dad is a has-been," the other boy yells.

"At least he isn't a used car salesman," the next kid offers up.

There is smoke everywhere. The toddlers, who are probably the real attendees of the event, are cuddled close to their mothers lining the sidewalk. The older kids appear to be going off the rails. Despite that, a group of dads still work two grills while several others stand, grumbling, further down from the first.

"I wish there was a video of what went down," one of the probies whispers in my direction as we start the hose to soak the piñata and jungle gym it is attached to, which is also now catching fire.

"Be careful, or you'll get the dessert table—" A shriek punctuates the sentence as we turn to see the fire hose promptly taking out the table.

There is now frosting spewed on the back fence, candle raindrops falling from the sky, and I'm staring into the very angry face of one Maya Glenn. That is not good news, as I'm pretty sure she thinks I'm public enemy number one, and to be honest, I'm not even sure why. We were all friends once upon a time, but in the years since Lane and I retired from the military and came home, the best greeting I had ever received from her was a snarl.

"What happened here?" I ask as the unreal scene imprints upon my brain.

"Oh, let's see," Maya says, crossing her arms and glaring in my direction. "I think we can safely say that male egos once again decided to spar for who could be the biggest jerk. One man's ribs were too salty, and another claimed that his wife liked them fine, which led to some conversation I would prefer not to repeat, and then the grill went into the bushes."

"Okay." I turn to check the distance from them to the piñata. There is no way the grill sparks could reach it. I turn back to the hanging T. rex piñata.

"Oh, and the first guy's wife started the piñata on fire when the opposing man's wife took his side," Maya grumbles.

"I'm not sure how to even write that in a report," I mutter.

"I bet you'll figure it out, as this would be right up your alley, don't you think?"

"I'm sorry, which part? I'm a volunteer firefighter; I put fires out, not toss kindling on them."

"The ego part. Don't even try to tell me you don't have a story or two in your memory banks that started just this way," Maya spits at me and then stomps off in her pale ballet slippers as best she can on the slick grass.

"What did you do to her?" Lane questions, surprise in his tone.

"I have no idea, but you picked up on the fact she despises me, right?"

"Um, I picked up on that, and I'm not the brightest light, as you all like to say," a newbie recruit calls out from a few feet away.

"So, it's not just me," Lane whispers. "I thought I was losing my mind and that she had just cut ties with me in particular."

"You mean she's that rude to you as well?"

"Nah, but she definitely won't talk to me. Normally, she ignores me or walks across the street when our paths cross," Lane says as we continue to work side by side to ensure the fire is out.

"Weird, we were so close to her brother Stephen. So close that I would've called him a brother," I whisper with sadness seeping into every word. "I have at least twice considered approaching her and talking about her attitude, but then I thought maybe it was just grief. Today, though, that was rough. Not to mention it happening in front of people. Might be time to try to figure things out. Did you ever visit with her parents when we got back?"

Lane's frown deepened, and a white tension line outlined his lips.

"I did go to see them, as I wanted to pay my condolences, but they wouldn't open the door. I didn't want to worry you, and then we got so busy. I have to be honest; I just sort of let it go."

"I get that." I inspect the bushes to ensure the fire is well and truly extinguished. "I have given little time to anyone who isn't part of the company or one of the veterans needing my attention," I admit as we walk back toward the fire engine. "I feel bad that maybe we let something fester that could've been handled before.

I'll try to figure out what might be going on with Maya. I feel we owe it to Stephen to care for his family if there is anything we can provide."

"I agree. If anything comes up that I can help with, don't hesitate to let me know."

"Will do. When approaching Maya, I might need some armor, though, based on today's interaction."

"I bet you'll be able to find some charming way to win her over," Lane teases. "I thought there wasn't a soul you couldn't charm? That's what you keep telling us at the office."

"Yeah, for a game," I grumble. "Maya has grown into a force to be reckoned with and might be a bit tougher to crack with that hard outer shell she wears."

"Good luck," Lane quips with a slap on my shoulder.

I don't know what I will be walking into, and nothing makes sense as to why Maya is angry. It had been years since her older brother Stephen passed from a roadside IED while serving. He enlisted nearly eighteen months after Lane and me, and his death had been a tough loss for all of us. Hearing about him passing and not being able to come home to attend his funeral had been devastating. When I returned home to Briar Glen, I had gone to his grave but hadn't expressed my condolences to his family. I had been raw when I returned, and then the business took off. In hindsight, that was really just an excuse. I should never have allowed this space to continue to develop between us, and I am long past due on rectifying it.

(Click here to get Kissing my Best Friend's Brother)